WANTING MY
Best Friend

ELYSE KELLY

*Happy Reading!
♡ Elyse
Kelly*

WANTING MY BEST FRIEND

Copyright © 2020 Elyse Kelly

Cover Design: Cormar Covers

Editing: Pagan Proofreading

All rights reserved.

The unauthorized reproduction, transmission, or distribution of any part of this copyrighted work is illegal. No part of this book may be reproduced in any form or by any means without the express written permission from the author, except for the use of brief quotations in a book review.

This literary work is fiction. Any resemblance to actual persons, living or dead, events, or establishments is entirely coincidental.

ISBN: 9798488126756 (print)

WANTING MY BEST FRIEND BLURB

I'm in love with my best friend. And he has absolutely no idea...

There's no way to deny it, and there's no way to change it. I've been madly and deeply in love with Max my whole life. But he only sees me like a sister—just a girl that's followed him around since we were kids.

So, how do I tell him? Will it ruin everything? Will he feel the same way? What if he doesn't?

I'm moving on to the next chapter of my life and I need to tell him how I feel before it's too late. I've known this beautiful boy since the first grade, and we've been inseparable since the day we met. It's time to finally tell him that I can't live without him.

I just hope it doesn't ruin everything.

Wanting My Best Friend is a sweet, but steamy friends-to-lovers novella with a HEA!

ONE
NOELLE

My eyes blink slowly as the sun begins creeping in through my blinds. Taking a deep breath, I roll to my side to grab my phone from my nightstand to see what time it is—7:00 a.m. As I let out a big yawn, I realize this is the last day I'm going to wake up in this bed, in this apartment, on this campus, in this city. By tonight, I'll be back in Magnolia Springs, starting my new life.

Four years have gone by in a flash, and I have loved every minute of college life. When I walked across that stage yesterday, my heart almost exploded; I was so excited to finally receive my diploma. I am now a proud graduate with a degree in journalism. I can't wait to get back home and start my job as the full-time culture writer for our local magazine. But more importantly than that, I'm finally ready to tell my best friend, Max, that I'm in love with him. I have no idea how he's going to react.

Max has been my best friend, and the boy next door, since the first grade. I remember seeing the huge moving truck pull up to the empty house next to mine, followed by a big, white SUV. The back door opened, and a boy with jet black hair and dark eyes jumped out and began to curiously look around.

There I sat on my bike, waiting on the sidewalk, just watching him watch the moving guys begin to unload the truck. After a few moments, he turned and looked my way. Our eyes locked, and a slow smile began to spread across his face. For some unexplainable reason, I couldn't move. I just sat there on my bike, with a death grip on my handle bars, watching this adorably goofy kid walk towards me.

"I'm Max. What's your name?"

"Um, I'm Noelle."

"Do you live on this street?"

"Yeah," I said quietly. He just stood there, looking at me expectantly. "I... I live... um, I live next door."

"You're kinda quiet, huh?" he asked, tilting his head to the side. I could tell he wasn't judging me, just observing me. And for once, I didn't feel uncomfortable with a new person.

"Um, I guess so," I answered, fidgeting on my bike.

"Well, I like quiet. But I'm not so quiet. My mom says I talk too much, but I get it from her. My dad's quiet like you, though." We both looked behind him when we heard someone call out.

"Max, honey, who's your new friend?"

A beautiful woman walks up behind him and puts her arm around his shoulders. Next to my mom, she's the prettiest woman I've ever seen. She's petite with thick, waist-length, straight black hair and dark eyes like Max's. There's something about her eyes that is so mesmerizing.

And her skin is lightly tanned, reminding me of the soft sand at the beach. She speaks with an interesting accent; one that I've never heard before.

"Hi, Mom. This is Noelle. She lives next door."

"Hi, Noelle. I'm Kim. It's nice to meet you, honey." She reaches out to shake my hand.

"It's nice to meet you, Miss Kim," I answer her. "You're really pretty," I tell her, looking down at my shoes.

"Well, thank you. You're pretty, too." She looks down at Max and says, "Honey, why don't you play with Noelle while dad and I help the movers." Turning to me, she asks, "Is that OK, Noelle?"

"Sure," I say, lifting my shoulders in a shrug. She kisses Max on the top of his head and turns to go back to helping the movers.

"Your mom sounds different from you," I tell him, asking him without really asking.

"She's from Vietnam. My dad says he met her there, and loved her so much the minute he saw her, that he just had to bring her back home with him. I guess it's true because they're always doing gross stuff like kissing and hugging all the time," he explains, his nose scrunched in disgust.

"Kissing's not gross. She just kissed you on the head. And my mom kisses me and my brother all the time."

"Adults kissing is gross. I'm never gonna kiss a girl when I'm an adult."

"Yes, you will," I argue.

"No, I won't."

"Uh huh."

"Nuh uh."

"Who are you arguing with, Noelle?" I hear my brother, Dane, ask me. He walks over to me and Max, his two best friends trailing behind him. Asher and Christian are brothers, and they flank Dane on each side, both narrowing their eyes at Max. I can't explain why, but I suddenly feel very protective of Max. I push my kickstand down with my foot and get off my bike, walking over to stand next to him.

"This is my friend, Max," I tell the boys.

"Friend? Since when?" Dane asks.

"Since now. Jeez." I roll my eyes at my big brother, who is four years older than me. I jerk my thumb over my shoulder as I tell him. "He's moving next door." Dane just grunts an acknowledgment.

"Hi," Max greets them with a small wave and a smile.

"Noelle is my little sister. And she's very shy. So, if we find out you messed with her, you'll have to answer to all three of us. Got it?"

"You don't have to tell everyone I'm shy, Dane," I say quietly. "Mom says I'm getting better. And I'm not shy with Max. He's being nice to me."

"Well, he better be." He narrows his eyes and says to Max, "We'll be right over here in the front yard. You don't let anything happen to my little sister. Got it?"

"You can trust me. I promise I'll take care of her," Max responds, puffing up his little chest.

"I'm not a baby, Dane." Turning to Max, I say, "Really, I'm not."

"I know," he says with a crooked smile.

"C'mon, guys. Let's go throw the football before Mom calls us for lunch." Dane, Christian, and Asher walk back to our front yard and begin playing again. I step over to my bike, and toe up the kickstand.

"Wanna see my tree house?" I ask Max.

"You have a tree house?! That's awesome! Let's go!"

He takes my bike, pushing it for me, as he follows me through my yard. And just as he promised, he takes care of me for the next sixteen years.

TWO
NOELLE

"Sis, is everything packed and ready?" Dane calls out from the living room. He arrived early this morning with our mom to help me move out of my apartment. I've been sharing it for the last three years with Kristen, my roommate. We met freshman year and became pretty close. Other than Max, she's the person I've been closest to these last four years. She's also the only one who knows how I really feel about him.

Asher and Christian are here too, since they came down yesterday for graduation. Max's parents had to get back home early for a business dinner, so the boys agreed to help move Max's stuff back to Magnolia Springs.

"Yeah, I'm all set," I answer Dane.

"Where's Max?"

"He's still packing up his room, but it shouldn't take much longer. His room in the athletic dorm didn't give him much space to hoard a bunch of stuff."

"OK. We'll stay here and help you, but Christian can go help Max." Christian pulls his phone from his back pocket to shoot Max a quick text. A few seconds later, his phone pings with an address, indicating where Christian needs to go.

"Alright, guys, I'm going over to Max's. We'll catch up with y'all in a bit," Christian says, taking the truck keys from Asher and walking toward the door.

"Why are they all so freakin' hot?!" Kristen whispers loudly to me.

"Pardon?" I ask her.

"Your brother and his friends are gorgeous, girl!"

"Ew, those are my brothers, Kristen!" I hiss at her.

"Well, they are sexy as hell, especially Dane. I'd climb that mountain of sexy, chocolate man-meat any day!"

"Gross! Don't make me puke!"

"What?! It's true."

"I don't wanna hear about it," I tell her while I shuffle the boxes in the kitchen. Dane and Asher are taking boxes to the truck, while Mom is cleaning my bedroom. Kristen is staying behind, as she's decided to go to grad school, so at least we don't have that much to clean up before we go.

"Fine, you don't want to talk about that, then let's talk about Max."

"There's nothing to talk about."

"Bullshit, Noe! You promised you were gonna tell him. Are you?"

"Yes... no... I don't know. I'll tell him when I'm ready."

"You said you were ready last night."

"You can't believe what I say when I've had wine. That doesn't count," I huff, moving around her as she stands at the kitchen island, not really helping.

"You have loved that boy your whole life. You need to tell him," she says, bumping me with her shoulder. "Or one day, you're gonna miss your chance and some other girl will snatch him up."

Jealousy runs through me at the thought of Max with another girl. He's not mine, so being jealous is irrational, but I feel it just the same. Kristen must be able to read the emotion running through me and places her hands on my shoulders, trying to calm me down.

"Look, girl. You know I love you, so I'm not trying to upset you. I know you're shy and nervous, but you're different with him. When you're around him, you practically glow. I know you have the confidence somewhere in there, so be brave and tell him how you feel."

"He sees me like a sister, not a girlfriend, Kristen. He always has." I let out a deep exhale. "He's so smart, and beautiful, and athletic, and talented, and popular. I'm just the quiet, adorkable girl that he likes to hang out with."

"Are you freakin' insane?! You are hot, Noe! Your skin is like perfectly smooth milk chocolate and your hair is always on point. You have the best smile on campus and the prettiest eyes. And I'd kill for just half your curves!

"You seriously can't tell me you haven't noticed all the guys that check you out, anytime we go anywhere. They practically drool when you walk by. And what about Kevin? I'm pretty sure that boy was in love with you."

"That boy was in lust with me and I wasn't having it. I only agreed to go out with him, to see if I could move past this insane crush on my best friend. We only went out a few times, but every time we did, it just didn't feel right. It just... felt... wrong," I say, shaking my head.

"It felt wrong because he wasn't Max," my mom says, sneaking up behind me.

"Mother! We're you listening?!" I ask, mortified.

"Calm down. I wasn't eavesdropping; I was just coming to get more cleaning supplies and overheard you." She rolls her eyes at me while Kristen laughs.

"And what do you mean, 'he wasn't Max'?"

"It felt wrong with Kevin, because he isn't the boy you're in love with."

"Well... yeah," I answer, slightly confused at where she's going with this.

"Because you're in love with Max," Mom says casually. My eyebrows shoot up to the sky in surprise at her declaration.

"Why would you say that?"

"Are you denying it?" Kristen asks, quirking her eyebrow at me.

"So, you two are ganging up on me?"

"Who's ganging up on you? I want in," Asher says, strutting into the kitchen with Dane following behind him.

"What is this, an intervention?" I mutter. I am completely embarrassed to be talking about this with my family and my roommate. I'd give anything for the floor to open up so I could disappear right now.

"We're trying to get Noe to finally admit she's in love with Max and agree to tell him. Tonight," Kristen explains.

"Oh, I like that plan." Asher nods his head in agreement.

"It's about damn time." I whip my head to Dane, completely in shock at what he just said.

"You knew?" My heart is pounding in my chest, and my forehead is breaking out in a light sheen of sweat.

"Sis, *all* we know. The question is, does Max know?" I look around at their faces, as each one confirms they clearly know how I feel about my best friend.

"How long have you known?" I ask them.

"Um, since I met you both freshman year," Kristen says.

"I think I knew when you guys hit high school, and you went to every single one of his soccer games, even the away ones," Asher answers.

"Nah, man, it was middle school when she started taking extra snacks to school for him, so he wouldn't get hungry in class," Dane says, popping Asher on his shoulder. He nods his head in agreement. How did they know I was sneaking extra snacks for him? He was growing so fast and had practice every day. I just didn't want him to be hungry. Friends do that, right?

"Well, I knew the moment you brought that boy over to the tree house. You two played up there all day, then you cried and cried when he had to go home." My mom just laughs, remembering the time when Max and I were younger. My face heats as I remember how I cried myself to sleep because Max had to go home.

I must be in some alternate universe. That's the only way to explain what's happening right now. My family has known I've been in love with Max for years, and no one said anything. *Wait a minute. Does this mean Max knows?!*

"I don't think so, honey," my mom says. *Crap, did I ask that out loud?*

"Yes, Noe, you're talking out loud." Kristen rolls her eyes, as she shakes her head at me.

"You guys are freaking me out! It doesn't matter anyway. I'm just his best friend. Can we just finish up and get going?" I ask, trying to escape the kitchen.

"He's in love with you too, you know," Dane calls out to me, stopping me dead in my tracks. I turn on my heel, staring at my brother and willing him to tell me the truth.

"How do you know that?" I whisper, unable to speak any louder—my heart pounding as blood rushes through my ears. Dane walks over to me, wrapping his muscular arm around my shoulders.

"Because. I'm your brother. I know things. Trust me, you'll see," he says, dropping a kiss to my forehead.

They all go about finishing up, while I just stand there in shock, trying to wrap my head around the mortifying, yet enlightening conversation I just had with everyone. Could they be right? *Is Max in love with me, too?*

THREE
MAX

I don't know what it is about today, but it just feels different. I mean, it is different because I'm finished with college, I'm moving out of my dorm room, and I'm moving back home to Magnolia Springs. But it's more than that. I'm starting my new life. And I want to start it with her.

Noelle Kelly has been my best friend since the first grade. She's been by my side, every minute, of every day, for the last sixteen years. She was so shy and quiet when I met her, but over time, she's come out of her shell. She had to, to be around my loud ass. I've always been the popular, outgoing soccer guy—the life of the party. But not Noe. She was just the quiet, super-smart girl observing everyone in the room.

It was only a few months ago (when she started dating that ass hat, Kevin) that I realized I was in love with her. Honestly, I think I've always been in love with her. I was just too afraid to admit it—too afraid she didn't feel the same. What if it ruined our friendship? I couldn't bear to not have her in my life.

It's always just been me and her, neither of us dating anyone, both of us focused on school. Outside of that, her mind was on writing, and mine was on soccer. But don't think I didn't notice how gorgeous she is. As soon as we got to high school, all the guys started noticing her, too. Overnight, she filled out and shot up, her curves drawing male appreciation everywhere we went.

Noelle is simply stunning. She has the most beautiful, creamy chocolate skin that feels like velvet to the touch. She keeps her silky, black hair straight and just past shoulder-length, with a slight flip at the ends. With high cheekbones and full lips, Noe has a face any woman would kill for. Her smile would make any man drop to his knees. And her soulful eyes are the color of whiskey. Sometimes I get a little lost when I stare into them for too long.

But then, out of nowhere, she agrees to go out with Kevin. He's a slick one, that guy. He pretends to be all studious, so serious about journalism, and his education and career. He's really just a douche canoe trying to get laid. And he knows Noelle Kelly is the ungettable get.

Noe has turned down every guy that has ever asked her out, except Kevin. Why she said yes to that jerk, I'll never know. Thank God they only went on a few dates. It's like he went out of his way to rub it in my face every time he came to pick her up. And of course, I made sure to be at her apartment every time he came over. I wanted him to see my face, and to know that I'd be right there waiting for her when she got home. And she always came home to me.

She ended it after their third date, much to Kevin's surprise and my delight. She never told me why, just said it didn't feel right to her. The reason wasn't important to me, as long as I didn't have to kick his ass, and as long as she wasn't going to be his girlfriend. But that's when I realized I wanted my best friend. And no matter what, I was going to have her. I've waited long enough.

Now, we're both moving back home. We've graduated, and we're getting ready to start our new journey. Noe's going to be working at the magazine, and I'll be working at my dad's accounting firm. It's time for me to tell her how I feel. I'm not going to wait for the next "Kevin" to come around and steal my girl. A loud knock at the door shakes me from my thoughts, and I know it must be Christian coming to help me move out of my dorm room.

"Hey, man. You ready?"

"Yeah. I don't have much left. I sent some stuff back this morning with Mom and Dad."

"Alright. Let's get this done so we can help Noelle finish up."

We start grabbing the few boxes I have and begin loading the luggage cart, so we can take the elevator down to the first floor. As we start loading up the bed of the truck, Christian asks, "You ready to be back home?"

"Yeah, man, I am. I miss my parents a lot. My dad's my best friend, and I'm actually pretty excited to be working with him at his firm. It'll be weird living in the same town and not living with them. But my apartment is just around the corner from the office, so it'll be nice that I can walk to work, since I'm right downtown."

"Sounds good. What about Noelle?"

"She staying with her mom, until she can save up for a place. I tried to get her to move in with me, since I have an extra bedroom. She wouldn't even have to pay rent, because I would be paying it anyway, but she wouldn't listen. It just makes sense for her to stay with me."

"Sure, it does," Christian says with a chuckle.

"Pardon?" I ask him, confused.

"Whatever you gotta tell yourself, man."

"Dude, what are you talking about?" I say, as I stop moving boxes and give him my full attention. He notices and stops, too.

"Real talk?" he asks. I nod my confirmation

"Fine. When are you gonna tell her you're in love with her?" My mouth drops open and my eyes go wide as saucers. *How does he know?* I've told no one, not even my dad. He just quirks his eyebrow at me, daring me to lie. I open and close my mouth like a fish, stalling to find the words. "We all know you love her, just so you know." *What in the actual fuck?*

"I mean... of course, I love her. She's my best friend."

"Yeeeaaaaah," he draws out. "But I think it's way more than that, Max. Give it up, man. It's obvious." He just shakes his head at me.

"What do you mean?" I wrinkle my brow in confusion.

"You two are like fucking magnets. You're drawn to each other. Always have been. If I see one of you, I know the other can't be too far away."

"So? We're friends." I shrug.

"Uh, I don't touch my friends the way you do."

"What's that supposed to mean?"

"Dude, you're constantly touching her. It's like you need to feel her. I get it. I'd be the same way, if I were in love." He turns to load the last box into the truck, leaving me standing there, dumbfounded.

"Does everyone know? Does she know?"

"I'm pretty sure everyone, but her, knows. She hasn't figured it out yet."

"Her mom and Dane know, and they're OK with it?"

"Mama Addy loves you like a son, and you know it. Dane may talk a big game and give you shit, but he sees you like a little brother. He knows Noe is safe with you, and you'll always take care of her. You've been taking care of her since that first day you met her and promised you would."

"I'll always take care of her," I tell him, sincerely.

"I know, man. I know."

"Do... um... do you think—" I can't bring myself to ask.

"Yeah, man. You need to tell her. Don't wait for some other guy to beat you to it." I can't believe I almost did.

With that, we close up the truck and return the cart and my room keys to the front desk. I look at my dorm one last time, ready to say goodbye to this chapter in my life and hello to starting the next phase with my dream girl.

We finish getting Noelle all packed up and moved out of her place. After a bittersweet goodbye to Kristen, we grab a quick bite to eat, then get on the road to head home. I'd give anything to have Noe ride with me, so we could talk; but we both took our cars to college with us, so we have to drive them home separately. It doesn't matter, though. She's coming over tonight to help me get settled into my new place, and that's when I'm going to tell her how I feel.

FOUR
MAX

It's been a long ass day and I'm damn exhausted, but I push all that aside knowing Noelle will be here any minute. My mom is the best, having set this place up for me before she and dad came down for graduation. She made sure this place was move-in ready for me and even stocked the fridge. No matter how old I get, I'll always be her baby, and I'm damn proud to be a mama's boy.

On the way home, I called my dad. I wanted to make sure I had a chance to talk to him before he and mom left for dinner with his business partners and some new big-shot client. My dad really is my best friend and I needed his advice on how to handle my conversation with Noe tonight. Taking the opportunity to, once again, tell me how he met Mom, I just listened as my dad retold the story.

He told me about how he was studying abroad in Vietnam for a semester; and his first week there, he walked into a restaurant and saw the most beautiful girl he'd ever seen, standing behind the counter. She was talking to an older woman, who looked a lot like her, so he thought she was probably her mother.

Once they noticed him standing at the door, the beautiful girl came around the counter and offered him a seat at a nearby table. Unable to speak the language, he asked the girl if she spoke English. She gave him a big, gorgeous smile, then continued the conversation in English.

Dad said he was smitten from the very minute he laid eyes on her. She was beautiful with long, black hair, and creamy skin. Her delicate features and petite stature were a sharp contrast to dad's muscular build and 6'2" height. He asked her to join him for dinner, and they've been inseparable ever since.

"Dad, what made Mom so different that you just had to have her?"

"That's easy, son. Your mom was so vivacious, it just couldn't be contained. She wasn't reserved and conservative like her mother clearly was. That woman shot laser beams at me with her eyes all night. I did everything I could to win your grandma over that night, but she was having none of it. She didn't want her oldest daughter getting mixed up with some American that wouldn't be staying in the country long."

"So, what did you do?"

"I came back every night for dinner, showing both your mom and grandma I was serious. Your mom was just so full of life—the light to my dark, the joy to my sadness. She filled me up when I was empty. I knew I was gonna love her for the rest of my life. And I love her even more now than I did back then. She's my everything." I can hear the dreaminess in my dad's voice, and it makes me so happy to know how in love my parents still are today.

"So. You ready to tell me why you're really calling? I know it isn't to hear me retell the story of how I met your mom." I take a deep breath and let out a loud sigh.

"I need some advice, Dad." I pause for a moment to think about my next words. "I need to tell Noelle something, and it needs to be tonight."

"Oh, thank God! Finally!" *What the hell?!*

"Uh, what's that now?"

"Your mom will be so happy. You know how much she loves Noelle. She's been waiting for this moment for years, son. Years."

"What in the hell is going on?"

"You're finally going to tell her you're in love with her, right?"

"But I... how did you know?"

"Good grief, son. We're not blind. You think we don't know when our baby boy is in love?"

"But I didn't even know until recently. How did you know?"

"You look at Noe the way I look at your mom. You talk about her like the sun rises and the moon sets with her. You don't go anywhere without her. Of course, you're in love with her, you big dummy. Mom and I were just waiting for you to figure it out." For the second time today, I'm stunned. Literally, everyone knows, and I was the last to figure it out.

"Why didn't you tell me?"

"I'm sorry. Did you just ask me why I didn't tell you that you were in love with your best friend?" I don't respond. "Well, now, I'm starting to question that expensive education I just paid for."

"I had a full scholarship for soccer, Dad," I deadpan.

"You know what I mean. We knew you'd figure it out eventually. So, when you gonna tell her?"

"Tonight. That's why I'm calling. I know what I want to say, but I'm not sure I know how to show her I love her."

"That's easy, son. As her man, your job is to make her soar. Your love should make her fly. You do whatever it is you have to, so that every day she knows no one will ever love her, protect her, and build her up the way you do. Spend every day with her, like it's your last day together. Kiss her every day, like you'll never see her again."

"Wow, dad. That's some poetic shit, right there."

"What can I say, I have a romantic heart. Look, son, I gotta go. If I don't start getting ready for this dinner, your mom will have my ass. And I make it a point to never piss off your mom. You need anything else?"

"Nah, I'm good, Dad. Tell mom I love her. I'll see you guys tomorrow."

"I love you, son. I hope you know we're so proud of you. You're an amazing young man, and I'm so proud to call you my son." I swallow down the lump in my throat and blink my watery eyes.

"I love you too, Dad."

I finished the drive home in silence, just replaying our conversation. Now, I'm standing in my new kitchen, staring at the front door and waiting for my soulmate to get here. If I never have another day on this Earth, I need to make sure Noelle knows how much I love her.

FIVE
NOELLE

Standing under the hot spray of the shower, I let the water rain down on my shoulders and back, trying my best to relax my nerves before I go over to Max's new place. I finish my shower and step out into the steamy bathroom. I'm careful to leave my hair wrapped in my scarf and shower cap, so the humidity in the bathroom doesn't ruin it and make it frizzy.

Deciding I need a minute to cool down, I step into my closet and look for a dress I can wear tonight. I usually just wear jeans and a cute tee with some quirky, nerdy saying. But tonight, I want to pay a little more attention to how I dress, since it will be the night I tell my best friend how much I love him.

Just thinking about it fills my tummy with butterflies. He's been my best friend for so long, but I've been physically attracted to him for years. Who wouldn't be? Max is the most beautiful boy I've ever seen.

At almost 6'3", thanks to his dad's height and German heritage, he's lean and muscular, his body taut from hours in the gym and on the soccer field. He has his mom's thick, jet-black hair and dark brows with smooth, lightly-tanned skin. His lips are so perfectly full and that sharp jaw rounds out his stunningly beautiful face. Max could give any GQ model a run for their money; he's so gorgeous.

Just thinking about how sexy he is, and that natural swagger he has, makes my thighs clench in desire. I've never been with a guy before and never wanted to. The only man I've ever wanted is Max.

Even when I tried to go out with Kevin, it was just so I could see if maybe I could trick myself into getting over my feelings for him. But it didn't work. All I did, every time we were together, was compare him to Max. And I think I always knew, in the back of my mind, that I was only going to be another notch in the bedpost for Kevin, which did not sit right with me at all. Nothing about me being with Kevin felt right, and I knew then that I would always be Max's girl, even if he didn't know it.

I finish picking out my clothes for tonight, keeping it casual because after all, I am supposed to be helping him unpack and get settled in. I brush my teeth and touch up my hair. I never wear makeup so I just swipe on my favorite vanilla-flavored lip gloss and spritz on the perfume Max bought me for Christmas last year.

Ready to go, I grab my keys and purse and kiss Mom goodbye, before making the short drive downtown. As I pull on to Main Street, I notice there's a new business going in next door to Davis Auto, the garage Asher and Christian own. The big sign in the window says, "Coming

Soon! The Sweet Spot." I wonder if it's going to be some kind of bakery or something.

I park in the lot of Max's new place and pull down the mirror to check my appearance one more time. Deciding this is as good as it's gonna get, I pop in a piece of mint gum and head inside. Taking the elevator to the third floor, my hands begin to shake a bit with nerves.

Tamping down the butterflies in my tummy, I wipe my damp palms on the front of my dress and step off the elevator. I take a few deep breaths as I walk down the hall to the last door on the left; I close my eyes and try to relax before knocking.

I hear some shuffling going on before I hear him walking towards me. The chain rattles, and the deadbolt makes a loud click, before the door opens to reveal the most handsome face I've ever seen. There before me is my beautiful Max, a panty-melting smile spread across his face.

We stare at each other for a few moments, almost as if this is the first time we're seeing one another. Then his eyes take me in from head to toe and I swear, his gaze feels like fingertips caressing my sensitive skin. When his eyes lock with mine, I see something different there—something I've never seen before. *Is that desire, I see?*

"Come in, Noe. I've been waiting for you," he says, stepping back so I can walk through the door. Just as my bare shoulder brushes against his tee-covered chest, I hear him deeply inhale and my pussy clenches. "You're wearing my favorite perfume."

"I know." It's all I can manage to say in this moment,

when I'm feeling so out of my element but also completely at home, simply because I'm with Max.

"Are you hungry? I have your favorite."

"You do?" I ask, surprised.

"Yep. My mom's Pho with beef, bean sprouts, herbs, lime, and fresh red chilies. I know you haven't had it since we came home for Spring break, so I thought you'd like it tonight."

"You always take care of me."

"And I always will, Noe. Let me give you a quick tour, then we can eat. I need to talk to you."

"I need to talk to you, too."

"Tour first, then we eat, then we talk. OK?"

"Perfect."

He gives me a tour of his new place and I love it. It's two bedrooms with one bath, but it's so spacious and open. I hope after tonight, I'll be spending a lot of time here.

We eat our meal in comfortable silence with moments of easy conversation about our new jobs. He directs me to get comfortable in the living room, which is still filled with boxes, while he cleans up and packs away the leftovers from dinner. Carrying two beers, he joins me in the living room, before handing me one and sitting next to me on the couch.

"Alright, I told you I needed to tell you something, so I'm just gonna jump right in," he says, nervously.

"Actually, can I go first? It's kind of important."

"Mine is really, really important."

"Well, mine is probably the most important, so I should go first."

"Really, Noelle? What are we, five?"

"You started it," I tease him. "Besides, I know your mom raised you to always let a lady go first." He just rolls his eyes at me and laughs.

"Fine. The floor is yours, lady."

I set my beer on the coffee table and turn my body to face him completely. As soon as I look into his piercing, dark gaze, I'm done for—like being held under some kind of spell. I close my eyes, taking in a deep breath. When they open I feel his big, warm hand gently squeeze my knee, encouraging me to begin speaking.

"I... I don't know where to begin," I start, taking another deep breath and willing my racing heart to calm down. "You have been my best friend my entire life and you've always been there for me. You've never let anyone or anything hurt me. You encouraged me when I needed it, you coaxed me out of my shyness when we were kids, and you gave me confidence when I didn't have any.

"I can't imagine my life without you, Max. I've waiting so long to tell you this, afraid how you'd react, but I don't want to wait anymore. I... um, I..." Before I can say another word, his mouth is crashing to mine and I'm lost.

SIX
MAX

Listening to Noelle say those things to me made my heart beat ten times faster. I'm not a hundred percent sure where she was going with all that, but I'm pretty sure we're on the same page and she was just about to tell me she loves me. I just couldn't wait a second longer; I had to kiss her. And I kissed her like my life depended on it.

Bringing my hands up to the sides of her face, I tilt her head back and lick the seam of her mouth. Instinctively she opens for me, allowing me to slide my tongue in, and I explore her mouth for the first time. When she lets out a soft moan, I use all the control I can muster and tear my mouth from hers, resting our foreheads together. Looking deep into her eyes, I finally tell her how I feel.

"I love you, Noelle. I have always loved you, and I will always love you. There has never been and never will be another girl for me. You're it, baby. My one and only. Please, tell me you feel the same." She just nods her response. "I need to hear the words, baby."

"I love you, too, Max. More than you know," she whispers.

"I do know, babe. Because as much as I take care of you, you take care of me. It's just like my dad said—you are the light to my dark, the joy to my sadness. You fill me up when I'm empty. You're my everything, Noelle. And I'm not gonna wait for another guy to steal you away from me."

"Your dad said all that?"

"He's a pretty romantic guy, apparently."

"I love you, Max. I wasn't sure if you'd feel the same way, but I knew I had to tell you. I'm tired of hiding how I feel, and I knew it was now or never." She lifts her mouth to mine, giving me a sweet kiss.

"Will you stay the night with me? We don't have to do anything you don't want to. I just want to hold you. I need to feel your body close to mine."

"I wanna stay with you. Um... can we... can we go to your room?" My Noe is still the same shy, sweet girl she's always been.

"Let's go," I tell her, taking her hand and helping her up from the couch. I lead her back to my room, closing the door behind us before pressing her soft body against it. I want to go slow for her, but I've been waiting my entire life for this moment, and I can't wait a second longer. I may be inexperienced, but there's a lot you can learn on the internet, and I've been around way too many other athletes to be clueless. I have to have her now.

"I'm trying, baby, but I need you so bad right now."

"Don't make me wait, Max. I've been waiting all this

time to be with you. I've never been with anyone else. I've been waiting for you. Only you."

And just like that, my control snaps. The kiss I give her is frenzied and passionate. I couldn't stop this kiss right now if I wanted to.

Both of us needing to take a breath, I break away from her lips, kissing along her jaw and trailing my mouth along her delicate neck. My hips press into hers, and I know she can feel how hard my dick is behind the zipper of my jeans. I slide my hands down to her thick, luscious ass, massaging the mounds with my big hands. Reaching around to the backs of her thighs, I lift her legs up to wrap around my waist, using the door as leverage to keep us steady.

"Tell me you need me, baby. Please."

"You know I do, Max. I need you," she pants. I can feel the heat of her pussy through her thin panties as she grinds her core against me. Wanting desperately to make her feel good, I carry her to the bed and set her down on the edge. She whines at the loss of contact, but I know I need to slow us down or I'll never last.

I drop to my knees before her, making us eye level. "I need to tell you something," I say between kisses.

"What is it? Can it wait?"

"I've never been with anyone else either, Noe. I've been waiting for you, too."

"You're perfect, Max," she says, giving me the sweetest smile.

"No, baby, you're perfect. But don't worry, I'm gonna take care of you. You may be my first, but that doesn't mean I don't know some things." I wiggle my eyebrows at her, playfully.

"I love you so much, Max," she says with a giggle. "And I trust you to make this good for me. Good for us."

"Damn, you're perfect," I tell her, before crashing my mouth against hers.

I slide my hands up her smooth thighs, under her dress, and up to her hips. Bunching the fabric of her dress in my hands, I tug it up and over her head, discarding it on the floor. Immediately she reaches for my shirt, and I help her remove it. She unclasps her bra, letting the straps slide down her arms, before slowly removing it from her body. I know how shy my girl is, but I want her to know how beautiful her body is to me.

"You're so gorgeous, baby. Every inch of you is beautiful." I shower her skin with kisses, trailing down to her perfect tits. My mouth waters at the sight of them. I take one of her puckered nipples into my mouth, and the moan she releases almost sends me over the edge. I gently push her back to rest on her elbows, as I kiss my way down the rest of her body.

She still has her panties on, and I can see how wet she is for me by the damp satin clinging to her pussy lips. I lower my head to the apex of her thighs and deeply inhale her scent. She smells fucking amazing. I take a long lick up the front of her panties, and her hips jerk in response.

Unable to wait a second more, I tear at the skimpy strings holding her panties to her body, ripping them apart and removing them. She gasps in shock at what I've done, but I just smirk at her, daring her to say something.

She rolls her eyes and shakes her head, as if she'd expect anything less from me.

Now that I finally have her naked, I lift her legs, resting her feet on the edge of the bed—far enough apart to fit my broad shoulders between her thighs. So many things I've been dreaming about doing to my girl, but those things will have to wait. It's our first time, and I want to make this good for her. So, I'll take it slow tonight, and we can try some new things later on.

I lift my hands to frame her pretty little pussy, my thumbs pulling her lips apart and putting her on display for me. I can see the rise and fall of her chest pick up, and I know she's nervous. But she doesn't stop me, her trust in me making my chest swell with pride.

"Just relax, babe. I promise you'll like this." I begin licking her pussy, and it's the sweetest thing I've ever tasted. With long licks from bottom to top, I take my time enjoying the feel of her hot, pink core on my mouth and the taste of her sweetness on my tongue. Her thighs begin to shake and her hands spear into my thick hair, pulling my face closer to her center.

"I... oh... it feels so good, babe." It's the first time she's ever called me "babe", and I just want to hear her say it again and again. I bring my attention to her clit and begin furiously licking the hard, little nub. "I'm so close, Max." She begins to mewl while clawing at the sheets.

"Get there, baby. Cum for me, Noe," I tell her, rubbing her clit hard and fast. Two seconds later and she cums, her moans filling the room and making my dick ache. I lick up every drop of her cream, not wanting to miss a single part of this experience together.

When she floats back down, I begin licking her again, this time adding a finger to her tight hole. I know I need to get her ready to take me. At 6'3", my cock is proportionate to my size and I'd rather die than hurt her. I know some pain is inevitable, but I need to loosen her up as much as I can, so she won't be so sore later.

I graze my teeth across her clit, sliding two fingers deep inside her. I feel for the rough patch at her front walls, and when she screams out my name, I know I've found her G-spot.

I continue to brush my fingers back and forth across it, feeling her arousal slide down my hand and wrist. Scissoring my fingers gently inside her, I stretch her tight pussy, hoping it'll make it easier for her to take my big dick. I feel her start to roll her hips, knowing her next orgasm is getting close. Doubling down on her G-spot and clit, I make my movements faster and harder, sending her over the edge once again.

I lick her pussy clean, then kiss and nibble the inside of her luscious thighs. Tearing my mouth away from her gorgeous body, I stand, wiping my mouth with the back of my hand. I look down at her beautiful body, as she lays across my bed, her eyes closed in bliss.

I place a knee on the bed and steady myself on one hand, as I cup her face with my other and kiss her sweet mouth, forcing her to taste herself. She moans and my dick becomes impossibly harder, the teeth of my zipper imprinting on the skin. I pull away and straighten up, reaching for the button of my jeans. Noe sits up and gently grabs my hands, stopping them from moving.

"Let me. Please?" she asks, quietly. I could never deny

her anything. I try to hold perfectly still as she takes her time, unbuttoning my jeans and sliding them down my legs. I step out of them, kicking them to the side, as she hooks her thumbs into the waistband of my boxers. She looks up at me, silently asking permission, and I nod at her to continue.

Slowly, so painfully slowly, she slides my boxers down and my very hard, very swollen dick springs free. Her eyes immediately go wide, and it'd be comical if I wasn't afraid I was going to hurt her. Swallowing hard, she looks up at me.

"I don't think you're gonna fit," she says, biting her pillowy lower lip before cocking her head in an adorable expression of concentration. My poor girl looks like she's trying to solve a math problem.

"It'll fit, babe. I promise," I tell her, lifting her chin with my index finger. I lean down to kiss her concern away and she melts into my kiss. Cupping her face with my hand, I say, "Whatever it takes, Noe. I'm going to make this good for you."

SEVEN
NOELLE

Max has the most perfect dick I've ever seen. Well, not that I've ever seen one in person, but I imagine this is what perfection looks like. It's so long and thick; and so hard that it bounces with his movements, as he takes off his clothes. There's no way it's gonna fit.

"It'll fit, babe. I promise."

Looking into his beautiful dark eyes, I know with every fiber of my being, I can trust Max to make me feel good. He'd never do anything to hurt me. Just knowing I can let go, and let him take care of me, brings a certain peace to my mind and allows me to enjoy every second of this with him.

Feeling brave, I say, "I... I want to taste you." I look at his beautiful dick again, seeing the head glisten with precum, as it seeps out of the slit of his tip. He grabs his dick and begins to pump himself slowly, and my mouth waters.

"There is nothing more I want to see, than those pretty lips wrapped around my cock. But my dick aches to be inside you, Noe. I need to be inside you. Now," he says, squeezing his dick with a pained expression on his gorgeous face.

He reaches into the nightstand and grabs a condom. I can't take my eyes off him, as I watch him roll the condom down his hard length. I slide back onto the bed, moving up toward the headboard as he follows me, crawling over my body.

"I'm gonna make you cum again, then I'm sliding my fat cock inside your tight little pussy."

My face flames at Max's dirty words. I've never heard him speak like this, and every word only turns me on more. I close my eyes and my breathing picks up, just as Max leans in to whisper in my ear.

"You like it when I talk like this, don't you, baby?" I nod as my heart beats faster. "Words, Noe. I need to hear them from your pretty mouth."

"Yes. Yes, I like it," I pant.

"I love you so much, Noe. Feel what you do to me," he says, rubbing his hard length across my swollen pussy lips. He presses his mouth to mine, kissing me deeply, as he runs the head of his cock up and down my dripping wet slit. I let out a moan, feeling the blood rush to my pussy and causing the lips to ache.

"Please, Max. I need you," I whine. He slides his hand down my body, finding my clit and rubbing it in small, firm circles. He pinches it between two fingers and at the same time, gently bites the tender flesh of my neck. Needing more, I begin rolling my hips into his fingers.

Aware that I'm getting closer, he slides two fingers inside my tight pussy, and begins to pump in and out of me. Nibbling and kissing my neck while whispering filthy things in my ear, he keeps fucking my pussy with those thick digits until my vision darkens, and I cum on his hand with a loud moan. Slowing down his movements, he works me through my orgasm, kissing my cheek and along my jaw.

"Please, tell me you're ready for me now, Noe. I don't think I can wait any longer," he says, resting his forehead against mine.

"I need you inside me, Max," I tell him, looking into his eyes. I bring my hands up to cup his face. "I love you more than anything. I've always been yours. Show me you're mine, too."

"I am yours, Noe. In every way."

He lines up the tip of his dick and begins kissing me again. The head of his huge dick is barely inside me and I already feel so full. My body instinctively arches as he inches his way inside my tight pussy.

"Relax for me, baby. You're squeezing me so tight."

He rubs his thumb over my clit and I instantly melt into him. My body relaxes, and he slides a bit more inside me, before pulling out slowly. Shallowly pumping in and out, he continues to massage my clit, pinching and gently pulling on it until I cum again.

Just as I do, he pushes his hips forward with one smooth thrust, until he bottoms out inside me. The whole world stops and all the air leaves my lungs in one loud exhale. There are no words to describe this feeling and this moment.

There's pain, but there's also pleasure. And my heart is so full right now, simply because I'm sharing this moment with the man I love more than anything. He's stretching me so wide, and the pain makes my eyes pool with tears. But when I look up at him, he's watching me so carefully; and I can tell he's slightly tortured by seeing my tears. He bends down to kiss them away.

"I'm so sorry it hurts, baby. I tried to make it hurt as little as possible," he says, kissing all over my face. After a few seconds, the pain begins to subside. I bring my hands down his muscular body, and reach around to grab his very firm, very tight ass.

"I need you to move now, Max. Please?" I beg him, slightly tilting my hips to show him I'm ready.

He slants his mouth over mine, kissing me deeply as he begins to move slowly in and out. I start meeting his thrusts with my own, and he takes the cue to pick up his speed. The heat inside me is flaming wildly now, and every move he makes feels so incredible.

"I had no idea it could feel this good," I tell him honestly.

"It only feels this good because I love you so much, and you love me. I know it would never be like this with anyone else. Only you, baby. Only you."

He's making love to me more passionately now, and the sounds of our bodies slapping together heightens my arousal. I can feel it dripping from inside me, and I can hear how slippery I am every time he slides in and out. This is the most erotic moment of my life, and I'm so amazed I get to share it with this beautiful man.

"I need you to cum for me, Noe. Can you do that, baby? I'm not gonna last much longer."

"I'm so close," I tell him.

He begins rolling his hips, rubbing his body against my clit every time he enters me. His thrusts are hard and punishing; and after a few more pumps, I see stars as I cum, my abs contracting and my head dropping back to the mattress. Max goes harder and faster while I'm squeezing his dick as I orgasm, then I feel his body tighten before he cums deep inside me.

Lazily pumping in and out of me, we both come back down from our orgasmic high. He finally stops, still inside me, and rests his head on mine. We look into each other's eyes, just staring, but not speaking for several moments.

"One day, you're gonna be my wife, Noe. You're all I'll ever need in this life."

"I love you, Max. Forever."

EPILOGUE

MAX

One Year Later

Standing in the doorway of our bathroom, I watch as Noelle finishes her hair. I have the most beautiful girl in the world, and she actually agreed to marry me. Not that I thought she'd say no, I just can't believe how lucky I am that I get to marry this girl. My best friend. My everything. She catches me staring at her and turns to look at me.

"Did you need something, baby?"

Just watching her be so confident makes my dick hard. Over the years, she definitely came out of her shell, but she was still a little shy and quiet. But this last year, she's really come into her own, becoming stronger and more confident every day.

Hearing her call me "baby" may not seem like a big deal, but terms of endearment were hard for her in the beginning. Now they roll off her tongue with ease, and I crave hearing them from her as often as she'll say them.

She was also shy about touching me, but now she can't keep her little hands off me, even when we're in public.

I love seeing my girl grow, becoming more and more comfortable in her own skin. I can't wait for her to be my wife. I'm going to give her everything she's ever wanted, starting with her dream wedding.

"No, I didn't need anything. I just like watching my pretty girl get all dressed up."

"We're not late, are we? We can't be late to our own engagement dinner."

"If we're late, it's your fault. You're the one that couldn't keep her greedy little hands off me," I tease her. Her brows shoot up to the ceiling.

"If I remember correctly, you're the one that couldn't keep his greedy little mouth off me."

"Can you blame me? Your sweet pussy just tastes too good."

"Don't talk like that. You know it turns me on," she says, a shy smile covering her face.

"Does it, now?" I say, moving into the bathroom and stalking towards her. She turns so her luscious ass rests against the counter as I cage her in between my arms, resting my hands on either side of her. I can see her pulse quicken at the base of her neck.

"Stop looking at me like that. We have to go," she says, breathily.

"Let me make you cum again, and I promise we can go." She thinks about it for a few seconds.

"Just once? You promise?" I give her a panty-melting grin, making her roll her eyes in humor. I lean in, smelling my favorite perfume on her neck, before pulling her earlobe gently between my teeth.

"Just one more time before dinner, then I'm gonna make you cum all night, Pretty Girl." I feel her body quiver as I lick the shell of her ear. She nods her head in agreement.

I reach my hand down and slide up her dress. Playing with the edge of her silk panties, I begin to leave hot kisses along her neck. Moving her panties to the side, I slide my fingers up and down her slit.

"You're so wet for me, Noe."

"I'm always wet for you, Max. Only you."

Slipping two fingers into her wet pussy, I begin to fuck her with my hand. I'd give anything to rip her panties right off her beautiful body, but I know our parents are waiting for us, so I need to make this quick. I pump my fingers in and out of her tight pussy, using my thumb to massage her clit. Knowing what will set her off quickly, I nibble her neck while pinching her nipple with my free hand.

Instantly she cums like a rocket, and I feel her cream coat my fingers and slide down my hand. I rub soft circles over her pussy as her breathing slows back down to normal. When she finally catches her breath, I remove my hand from her panties and bring my fingers to my mouth to lick them clean. Nothing on Earth tastes as good as her pussy.

I lean in to her, resting my weight on my hands that are placed on the counter. She brings her hands to my face, pulling me in for a kiss. She's so turned on now;

kissing me deeply and pressing her hot body against my hard dick, which is still restrained by my pants.

"I'll give you more tonight, baby, when we get home. I promised you just once, remember?" I tease her. She gives me the cutest pout and I kiss her little nose. She sighs in mock frustration, then moves to the side so I can wash my hands.

Rubbing her hand up and down the length of my cock, she says, "Maybe we can make it a quick dinner? So I can give you what you've already given me. Twice."

"It's our engagement dinner with our parents. You know they'll talk and carry on forever. But maybe, if you're a good girl, we can sneak out before dessert."

"Deal." She turns to leave the bathroom, but I gently catch her wrist, pulling her body into mine.

"I love you, with all my heart and all my soul, Noelle. You are the light to my dark. The joy to my sadness. You fill me up when I'm empty. You're my everything, baby. You're all I'll ever need in the world."

"I can't wait to be your wife, Max. My best friend. My soulmate. I love you, baby."

She rises up on her tiptoes to give me a passionate kiss. I can't wait to marry my best friend.

THANK YOU!

From the bottom of my heart, thank you for reading my book! I'm just a true Southern girl, reading and writing books, asking you to love me. I hope my mix of romance, with a dash of swoon, and a pinch of smut brings a smile to your face and a tingle to your fun bits.

If you enjoyed my book, please consider leaving a review on Amazon, Goodreads, etc. Even if it's just a sentence or two about what you liked most about my book, it will help my work to be seen by other readers.

HAPPY READING!

FIND ELYSE KELLY AT:

Sign up for my **NEWSLETTER** to receive updates about upcoming releases, exclusives, giveaways, and more!
https://bit.ly/2WoABd5

AMAZON: https://amzn.to/36gI26a
BOOKBUB: https://bit.ly/3kgNpaY
GOODREADS: https://bit.ly/33aUAKn
TIKTOK: https://bit.ly/37L1SWU
INSTAGRAM: https://bit.ly/3izpaTh
FACEBOOK: https://bit.ly/3D2vSMc
EMAIL: elyse@elysekellybooks.com

OTHER BOOKS BY ELYSE KELLY:

THE MAGNOLIA SPRINGS SERIES

Welcome to Magnolia Springs! If you're looking for laugh out loud moments with lots of swoon and sexy book boyfriends, then you've come to the right place! All the books in this series are complete standalones featuring a different couple, each with a HEA! You can enjoy these books in any order.

THE SWEET SPOT

DON'T DATE YOUR ROOMMATE

MY FAKE BOYFRIEND

THE HEATED NOVELLA SERIES

Each book in The Heated Novella Series can be read as a complete standalone. These are fast, sexy, reads featuring hot alpha males that keep you nice and heated all the way through to the happy ending.

MAKING HER MINE

ALL FOR YOU

MORE THAN MONEY: BILLIONAIRE ROMANCE SERIES

13 authors contributed individual books to the More Than Money Series, each of which can be read as a complete standalone. This series will have you swooning over these sexy billionaires with big wallets and even bigger hearts!

So, grab a fan and a cool drink, because it's about to get hot in here!

MR. ARROGANT: A BILLIONAIRE ROMANCE

KISMET COVE SINGLES WEEK SERIES

Eleven authors are bringing eleven brand new stories about finding love in all sorts of way and how the charm of this lake town brings people together. Known for its delightful allure, Kismet Cove is the perfect background to find the one!

TRIPPED UP

ACKNOWLEDGMENTS

To my amazing family, thank you for supporting me and each and every passion I've wanted to pursue. You always encourage me to do whatever makes me happy and I'm so grateful to have you all. I love you and I hope I make you proud each and every day.

To my author friends who provide invaluable advice and an offer to be my sounding board, thanks for EVERY-THING! I would never have been brave enough to pursue my passion without you, and I would have no clue what I'm doing without your help along the way.

To Kat thanks for helping me make this the most amazing manuscript for my readers! You guys not only help me make my books better, but your support is beyond anything I could have ever expected.

To my A Team, thanks for listening to me drone on and on about all the books I read and all the books I'm writing. You guys are the best.

To all the readers, bookstagrammers, and bloggers, thank you for reading, reviewing, and promoting my books. I wouldn't be here without you and I'm so thankful for each and every one of you.

THE Sweet SPOT

Turn the page for a sneak peek at
BOOK 1
THE MAGNOLIA SPRINGS SERIES

THE SWEET SPOT

Copyright © 2020 Elyse Kelly

Cover Design: Sarah Kil Creative Studio

Editing: Pagan Proofreading

All rights reserved.

The unauthorized reproduction, transmission, or distribution of any part of this copyrighted work is illegal. No part of this book may be reproduced in any form or by any means without the express written permission from the author, except for the use of brief quotations in a book review.

This literary work is fiction. Any resemblance to actual persons, living or dead, events, or establishments is entirely coincidental.

ISBN-13: 979-8685473103 (print)

ONE
CALLIE

It's finally happening! I can't believe it's finally happening! This is legit my life right now! Holy shit, I'm so excited!

When I told my parents I was moving to Georgia, they both looked at me like I sprouted a magic unicorn horn and pink hooves. They've always known I wanted to open my own specialty bakery and they have been the most supportive parents a girl could ask for. They just thought I wanted to open my bakery in our hometown in Tennessee. I never mentioned moving and I certainly didn't mention moving so far away.

I lived out of state for a few years when I went to culinary school, but ever the good daughter, I came home monthly and promptly moved back right after graduation. I've been working at a bakery back home for two years, learning the ropes and saving my money. But now it's time for this baby bird to leave the nest. I hate to leave my parents, but I'm ready to start my own life and I'm ready to do it in another town. *Deuces!*

So here I am! Finally living in Magnolia Springs,

Georgia, just outside of Savannah and I. LOVE. IT! This is the cutest town EVER! I feel like I'm living in one of those made-for-TV romance movies. It's a small town with only about 20,000 people, but it's perfect. Everywhere you turn there's a smiling face. You can drive down any street and someone will wave at you as you go by. Everyone speaks to you, even if they don't know you. And there's even a Main Street with cute shops and boutiques, family-owned businesses, and now a cupcake shop. *You're welcome, Magnolia Springs!*

I'm about a week out from the grand opening of The Sweet Spot. Somehow, I convinced my bestie Ava to move with me and help me open the bakery. I don't think this is exactly what she planned to do with her life, but she loves me and I could tell she was running away from something back home. Though I'm not sure what that something is, at some point, I'll get to the bottom it. Ava has been my BFF since kindergarten and there is no way I could live without her. So, when I saw she needed to get away, I dragged her with me to open The Sweet Spot.

I've only been in town for a few weeks, getting the shop ready, and settling in to our cozy little home. Today I'm working on promoting our grand opening, so I've whipped up some cupcakes to take to the other businesses on Main Street. There's a mechanic's shop on the left side of my bakery, and a trendy clothing boutique to the right. There're other businesses as you go down the street, so I'll try to hit those up later today, too. Far be it from me to deny anyone a chance to get free cupcakes.

Sophie's is the cutest boutique I think I've ever set foot in. The clothes are amazing and there's also little trinkets, gifts, home goods, and a ton of other stuff. You can tell this is the kind of place someone has poured a lot of time and love into. You can't help but feel happy as soon as you walk in. The front door chimes softly as I open it, signaling my entrance.

"Hi, there! I'll be with you in just a sec." I hear called from somewhere in the store.

"No worries. Take your time." I take a look around, being careful not to drop the box of a dozen cupcakes I'm holding. Ava would love this place. We'll definitely be back here soon to drop some cash. Gotta support local businesses! After a few minutes, I hear someone approaching me.

"Hi, I'm Sophie. I think I've seen you around. You're new in town, right?" Sophie looks to be about my age. She's beautiful, with milk chocolate hair and striking green eyes. I'd kill for her complexion. She looks very boho chic, but in an effortless way - kind of like Stevie Nicks. She's dressed in a high-waisted hi-lo skirt that ties at the middle and a simple baby pink t-shirt tucked into it.

"Yeah, I'm Callie. I'm opening The Sweet Spot next door. I hope we haven't disturbed you too much with our remodeling the last few weeks."

"Not at all. I'm happy to see someone moving in, now that the Johnsons have retired and moved to Florida."

"Well, I hope you like cupcakes because these are for you. Our grand opening is this Saturday so I thought I'd bribe you to come check out my shop, with some awesome goodness right here."

"You had me at cupcakes!" she says with widened

eyes. I open the box to let her see how amazeballs I am at baking cupcakes. Yeah, that's right, I'm not afraid to toot my own horn!

"These smell like unicorn dreams and rainbows!" I think she's actually drooling now. I try not to stare as she's eye-fucking my cupcakes like she's thinking dirty thoughts. Hell, I don't know this girl. Maybe she is thinking dirty thoughts. *You do you, girl!*

"Uh... should I maybe give you some alone time with those?"

"Gah! Sorry! Didn't mean to be so awkward. These just look and smell so amazing that I had a moment of insanity. Thanks for bringing these by! I can't wait to try them!"

"I hope you like them. And maybe you could mention to your customers there's an awesome new cupcake bakery opening next door?" I ask hesitantly as I clasp my hands behind my back and dig the toe of my converse into the floor.

"Oh, you got it! I'm excited to see someone my own age around here. I grew up here and a lot of kids move away for college and don't come back. The town's mostly parents and grandparents, and nosy ol' busy-bodies that stay all up in your business. It's quiet and low-key around here, but there are no secrets safe in Magnolia Springs. Just keep that in mind.

"Truth be told, I've known about you since the day you got here. The gossips in town couldn't wait to tell everyone about the new girl. And apparently you have a roommate? You guys are renting the Watson's house on Dogwood, right?"

"Well shit, I guess there really are no secrets here. My bestie Ava and I moved here from Tennessee about six weeks ago."

"Oh, I know. Like I said, no secrets. But don't worry, you'll love it here. Everyone is super nice, even if they are a bit nosy and gossipy. Just steer clear of Stacy Trent and her Misfit Toys. They're our age but still living in their high school days, wearing pink on Wednesdays and thinking life is the extended cut of Mean Girls. A gorgeous girl like you will definitely be on their radar."

"Thanks for the heads up. I've known my fair share of mean girls, so I think I can handle 'em. Well, I've got another delivery to make. I hope we can hang out soon. I could always use a new friend in town." She claps her hands and jumps up and down like she's on *The Price is Right*.

"Yes! I'll definitely be your Magnolia Springs tour guide!" I grin at her, thinking to myself, "This girl is too much." I give her a quick hug, 'cause I'm a hugger, and tell her I'll see her soon. I make my way back to the shop to pick up another box of cupcakes to deliver to the auto shop next door. If they're half as friendly as Sophie, I know I've made the right decision to move here.

TWO
ASHER

I just wrapped up putting a new alternator on the Honda Odyssey minivan Mrs. Smith dropped off this morning. I don't know how she manages with five kids, but if I can help keep her moving while she carts around her own personal basketball team, it's the least I could do. Her husband works out of town a lot, so she's definitely got her hands full with those hellions of hers.

I wipe my greasy hands on the rag I keep in my back pocket and smooth my hair off my face before replacing my favorite hat backwards on my head. I walk out to the front of the shop to write the ticket for Mrs. Smith, but I stop dead in my tracks just before I open the glass door that separates the front office from the body shop.

Well, fuck me to the moon and back! Who is SHE?! I quickly close my gaping mouth as my dick begins to tingle before I open the door to find out who this goddess is. She hasn't noticed me yet, so I take a moment to appreciate the girl in front of me, as she's looking around my lobby, unaware of my presence. She has the most beautiful, light caramel skin with long, curly black hair that I bet would feel so soft wrapped up in my fist. Curves for days and an hour-glass figure that makes me wanna drop to my knees and motorboat her tits. Her banging body is all woman with an ass that puts a Kardashian to shame. My favorite part though, is that she's dressed in a vintage Weezer t-shirt, dark blue skinny jeans that look painted on her luscious body, and black converse on her cute little feet. *It's about to be on like Donkey Kong!*

Just as I get ready to open the door to the woman of my dreams, a hand claps me on my shoulder. My best friend, Dane, who works at the shop with me and my brother Christian, lets out a low whistle and asks, "Where's she been all my life?" Before I can think straight, I shuck off his huge hand and blurt out, "Mine!" Then quickly I open the door. I walk toward the front desk with Dane hot on my heels, chuckling under his breath and shaking his head at me. She turns to me and Dane, holding a hot pink box in her hands like it contains a prized possession.

"Hi, I'm Callie!" she says brightly, in a voice that could only come from an angel. Dane is quick to reach out from where he's standing behind me and offer his hand.

"I'm in love!" Dane tells her with a smile. "I'm Dane, by the way. And this is Asher." She giggles softly as her cheeks turn a soft peach flush. Damn, is that sexy! And she's not even trying.

"I'm Asher," I say like an idiot. Shaking my head, I inwardly cringe. *Real smooth, Asher, real smooth.*

She smiles at me sweetly. "So, he said. Here, these are for you." I take the box from her hands and open it to see the most mouth-watering cupcakes I've ever seen. Each one, a different flavor with mile high frosting on top.

"You wanna be my wife?" Dane says to her as he drools over the cupcakes from over my shoulder.

I nudge him in the ribs. "These are mine and I'm not sharing." He gives me a mock affronted look and pouts. "But I'm your best friend!"

"Now now, boys, sharing is caring," she chastises us jokingly. She winks at me and my dick that I willed to calm down earlier is now trying his damnedest to get to her. She looks at me with these soul-stealing, sterling silver eyes and I know I've got to get it together before I fall all over her. *You're better than this, Asher!*

"My cupcake shop, The Sweet Spot, opens next week. Our grand opening is Saturday. We're neighbors!" I can't take my eyes off her lips as she's speaking.

"So... can I bribe you guys with these cupcakes and get you to come to the grand opening? Maybe tell all your customers about my new place?" she says, looking up at me through her long, black lashes.

"I'll be there on one condition." I give her my best mega-watt smile. She may be new in town, and maybe she's affecting my dick more than any woman ever has before, but I'm Asher Davis. No woman has ever said no to this smile and these dimples. I cock my head to the side and look deep in her eyes, "Go out with me."

That sweet peach blush is back and she bites her pillowy lower lip, but then she gives her head a subtle shake like she's clearing a fog from her brain.

"Hmmmm... maybe another time."

"Damn, son! That has never happened before!" Dane

says exactly what I'm thinking, covering his mouth with his fist and laughing behind me. Maybe she misunderstood me. Right? *Who would turn down these dimples?*

"What's that now?" I ask her surprised, my eyebrows almost at my hairline.

"I just have a lot on my plate, opening the bakery right now." She lifts her shoulder in a slight shrug. Gaining conviction, she says, "And besides, you have 'heart-breaker', 'panty-melter', and 'trouble-maker' written all over you. My mama told me all about boys like you." She quirks her eyebrow, daring me to tell her it's not true. So, what if it's true? She doesn't know that. Yet.

"And just what did your mama say about boys like me?"

"Wouldn't you like to know," she says. "I've got to get going. It was nice to meet you. See ya, boys! Enjoy the cupcakes! They taste as sweet as they look." With a parting wink, the little minx sways her sweet hips right out the front door.

"I'm giving you one chance with that girl, before I'm all over that." I cut my eyes at Dane and punch him in the arm, letting him know that little Miss Callie is all mine.

A second later the front door chimes and Christian walks in, letting out a loud wolf whistle. "Did you guys catch the hottie outside?"

"Mine!" I say, like some kind of caveman that wants to club her over the head and drag her back to my cave. I don't know what it is about this girl that's gotten my full attention, but she has it. And I'm not settling for a no.

Okay, my little cupcake. You wanna play hard to get? Well, game on, baby. I love a good chase.

THREE
CALLIE

I. AM. SCREWED! I can't squeeze my thighs together tight enough to relieve the sexual tension I'm feeling in my lady bits right now. That man is sex on a stick! Walking, talking, breathing sex. Sweet mama, am I in trouble.

That is the most gorgeous man I've ever seen. So tall and muscular, his body lean and built from hours of physical labor. Thick dark hair pulled back under a backwards hat. Cerulean blue eyes that demand your attention. And those dimples! That man definitely leaves a wake of exploded ovaries everywhere he goes.

And his friend Dane is just as hot! Gotta be over six and a half feet of sexy chocolate, and built like a Mack truck with muscles on top of muscles. Black hair close-cropped, with scruff that begs to be rubbed against a woman's bare skin, and a smile that drops panties within seconds.

Then I almost run over hottie number three when I walked out the door. He looked a lot like Asher, but with blond hair and no dimples. I'd bet they were brothers with how similar they look. He had a sexy swagger about him too, as he came strutting through the door. *What are they putting in the water here?!* Those three boys are nothing but living, breathing sex gods!

I barrel into The Sweet Spot and quickly lock up. I've gotta get away from all that sexiness before my ovaries faint! I close the back door and make my way to my black 4Runner, hoping I don't run into Captain Sexy himself.

As fate would have it, I am not that lucky. Cursing my luck, I keep my head down and dig into my bag for my keys, feeling his stare across the small back parking lot. I spot Captain Sexy leaning against the trunk of a blue minivan, his legs crossed at the ankles, and his huge tanned arms crossed over his broad chest. I try not to stare but my mouth waters looking at the full sleeve he has inked on his left arm, just begging me to take a lick.

He catches me staring, while I almost walk right into the back corner of my SUV. Way to be cool, Callie! I hear him call out to me, "Hey, Cupcake! Be seeing you soon." Then the cocky bastard winks at me and my panties catch fire. I have got to get home before I embarrass myself any further.

The short drive home — curse this town for being so small — did nothing to calm my libido. Even with the A/C on full blast, my skin is still hot all over. *What has that man done to me?* If I'm feeling like this after one brief encounter, I'll never survive an actual date. I can't believe I told him "no" when my lady bits were screaming "hell yeah". I walk in the door and drop my stuff down on the table. I hear Ava in the kitchen and rush in to tell her all about my brush with hotness.

"Everything go OK at the shop today?" Ava's standing in the kitchen, drinking a glass of sweet tea and looking through the mail. My bestie is so pretty with golden blond hair, baby blue eyes, and a runner's body I'd kill for. Why she's still single, I'll never know.

"Sure! If you count running into the three hottest guys on the planet, then yes, everything was great at the shop today."

"Three hottest guys? In this Podunk town? Spill," she says in disbelief.

"Hey, I love this town! You're gonna love it too. Just wait."

"Yeah, we'll see. Now, tell me about these hotties and quit stalling."

"Fine," I tell her with feigned exasperation. "After I dropped cupcakes off to Sophie's Boutique, which you're gonna love BTDubs. Sophie is a real sweetheart and her shop has some amazing stuff.

"Anyway, I then dropped some off at Davis Auto next door. Let me tell you, that is the place where all panties go to melt and ovaries go to combust. No joke, extreme sexiness must be a requirement to work there because those boys scream sex god."

"Well, well, well, little Miss I Don't Have Time to Date. Sure seems like you're interested in dating now, huh?" she says with a smirk.

"I don't have time to date, but I'm not blind. Or dead. There is nothing wrong with examining the merchandise," I say with a small shrug, pretending to be unaffected.

"You know I've known you since kindergarten, right? I can read you like a damn book. You are seriously swooning right now. I can hear your uterus sighing dreamily while your hoo-ha does jazz hands."

I toss a throw pillow at her. "Shut up! If you saw these guys, you'd be acting the same way. You'll see what I mean when you meet them."

"Can't wait," she deadpans. "I need to get my feet wet in this town anyway."

"Oh, is that what you're getting wet? I thought it was something else." Now it's her turn to throw a pillow at me. "What's for dinner anyway? I'm starved."

"Do I look like your personal chef?" she asks me with a cocked brow.

"No, you look like my best friend who loves me and wants to feed me after a long day at the bakery." I give her my best pout with extra sappy puppy dog eyes for good measure.

"Girl, those eyes don't work on me. I invented that look." Damn it, she's right. No one gives a pout better than Ava. I've seen grown men fall to their knees to please her with just one pout.

"Fine, let's go get a pizza. I'm done working in kitchens for today." I grab my keys, putting my debit card, driver's license, and favorite lip gloss in my pockets, and head for the door.

Ava and I are jamming out with the windows down when we pull into the cute little pizza place in town, Big Mike's. Starving, we both jump out of my SUV and make our way into the restaurant. It's a small mom and pop place with red checkered tablecloths and big comfy booths. It smells like cheesy garlic heaven and has pictures of family and locals donning the walls.

I come to a complete stop when I open the front door. *Well, fuck sticks! If it isn't Captain Sexy again and his Merry Band of Panty-Melters.* Determined to show him that he has no effect on me — even my vagina coughs a "yeah right" at me — I head straight to the hostess stand.

"Just two?" the tall drink of teenage awkwardness asks me and Ava.

"Just two, please." I throw in a "sweetie", hoping to make him less nervous. Clearly, he's smitten with Ava and can't help but ogle her. Who can blame him? Ava's gorgeous. I'm quietly hoping he'll take us to any table that isn't near Team Hottie, but again that bitch Fate is out to get me.

"Is this table OK?" He takes us to one just a table away from the three most gorgeous men I've ever seen.

"It's fine, honey, thanks," I tell him, secretly wishing he'd move us. He hands us two menus and promises to be right back to take our drink order.

"Who is the table of deliciousness that keeps looking over here?" I pretend not to hear Ava and keep staring at my menu, reading absolutely nothing, just staring at the words.

"Girl, I know you heard me. Are those the guys that had you creaming your panties earlier?"

"Sweet Jesus, would you keep your voice down," I hiss at her. Before I can say anything else, Captain Sexy comes strutting our way. That man has swagger for days. Those thick thighs, corded forearms — every girl loves arm porn — and the most stunning blue eyes I have ever seen. He smells so masculine like broken hearts, bad decisions, a damn good time, and a hint of motor oil.

"Uh, Callie? You got... a little bit of something right there," Ava says, implying I'm drooling, which of course I'm not. Am I? I furiously blush and kick her under the table.

"Aren't you gonna introduce me to your friend, Cupcake?" Asher asks me.

"She's so rude. I'm Ava. And you are?" she pretends to be demure and gingerly offers him her hand. Of course, I roll my eyes at her theatrics.

"I'm Asher, Cupcake's date later this week. That's my friend, Dane, and my brother, Christian," he says, pointing to the other Hotties.

"Please don't call me 'Cupcake'. And we're not going on a date."

"So your mouth says, but your body says something else." He's totally right, but I'm not giving in just yet.

"You have no idea what my body's saying," I lie. Seductively, he leans into me, his hot mouth just barely brushing the shell of my ear. I feel the warmth of his body so close to mine. My heart pounds in my chest and my breath quickens as he whispers so only I can hear.

"I know exactly what your body's saying, sweetheart. Don't fight it. I can tell you want me just as much as I want you by the way you're holding your breath right now. I can see your pulse at the base of your delicate neck picking up. I can feel the heat radiating off you in waves right now." He gently brushes the back of his knuckles against the bare skin of my arms and I break out in goosebumps. "If I could touch that sweet pussy of yours right now, I bet it'd be wet for me." *Holy fuck balls!!!* "You promised it'd taste as sweet as it looks, right?" He pulls back and smirks, knowing the effect he has on me. *Smug Bastard!*

"I don't know what that man said to you, but judging by your reaction, I think I'm gonna go sit at the other table with Dane and Christian." I glare at Ava, willing her to stay, but that bitch just keeps walking. *Best Friend my ass!*

"Well, Cupcake, now that we're alone..."

"This is still not a date. Just a coincidence that we ran into each other." I try to shake off the lust coursing through my body.

"Eh, I think it's fate. Give it up, Cupcake, you're gonna be mine sooner or later." He says, leaning back in his chair, all man spread and gorgeous.

"Why? Because every other girl throws her panties at you, the second they get a glimpse of those dimples and all that sexiness?"

"Aw, babe, you think I'm sexy?" *Damn it, Callie!* "I think you're sexy too. And the way you blush makes me think you don't even know just how sexy you are." I can feel my cheeks getting hot again. "See what I mean."

"Alright, look. I'm starving and it's been a long day. I'm too tired to fight your pitiful attempt at hitting on me. The least you can do is feed me while my defenses are down." I lift my chin in defiance, a poor effort at acting like I'm not gonna give into this man in the very near future. But he doesn't know that.

"Pitiful attempt? Keep telling yourself that, Cupcake. You know you're gonna be mine sooner or later, but I'll let you run for now. Anything worthwhile is worth the chase."

The Sweet Spot is available now!

Made in the USA
Monee, IL
22 October 2021